GHOST HUNTERS

and the
GRUESOME
INVINCIBLE
LIGHTNING
GHOST!

Dear Ghostfans

Where are the most unlikely ghosts to be found? Hetty and her crew meet some hot horrid ones in a hotel, but my most surprising ghost lived in the greenhouse! He finished off my gardening at night, putting things right!

Where would yours be? Under the stairs. . .in the computer. . . under the bed! Whoa! Write and tell us at chickenhouse@doublecluck.com

Yours with a slight shiver!

Barry Cunningham
Publisher

GHOST HUNTERS

and the GRUESOME INVINCIBLE LIGHTNING GHOST!

by CORNELIA FUNKE

Chicken House

2 Palmer Street, Frome Somerset BA11 1DS

Original text copyright © 1994 by Loewe Verlag
English translation by Helena Ragg-Kirkby copyright © 2006 by Cornelia Funke

First published in Great Britain in 2007 by
The Chicken House
2 Palmer Street
Frome, Somerset BA11 1DS
United Kingdom
www.doublecluck.com

Cover design by butterworthdesign.com
Inside illustrations by Cornelia Funke © 1994
Inside design by Leyah Jensen
Printed and bound in Great Britain

1 3 5 7 9 10 8 6 4 2

British Library Cataloguing in Publication data available.

ISBN 978-1-905294-13-8

For
Marion
and
her
men

ALSO BY
CORNELIA FUNKE

DRAGON RIDER

THE THIEF LORD

INKHEART

INKSPELL

WHEN SANTA FELL TO EARTH

GHOSTHUNTERS
and the Incredibly Revolting Ghost!

CONTENTS

Let me introduce three of the most successful ghosthunters of our time.

Hetty Hyssop has been a world-famous expert in the field of professional ghosthunting for many, many years – and **Tom** and **Hugo the ASG** (Averagely Spooky Ghost) have been working as her assistants since they joined forces for their first and extremely dangerous case – namely, the successful capture of an **IRG** (**I**ncredibly **R**evolting **G**host), one of the most dangerous ghost species on this planet.

Since then, the name Hetty Hyssop and Co. has been famous for just what it says on their business cards: ALL TYPES OF GHOSTHUNTING UNDERTAKEN.

In fact, there's scarcely any ghost that could frighten our three experts nowadays. But the job we're going to hear about in this book was really hot stuff – quite literally – even for such experienced ghosthunters as Hyssop and Co.

So, I hope you're sitting comfortably in a brightly lit room – knowing that ghosts hate the light. And that you are wearing red clothes – knowing red is the most disturbing colour for ghosts – because here we go. . .

Just a Little Trip

It's always the same with dangerous adventures: they start off quite harmlessly.

One fine autumn day, the famous ghosthunter Hetty Hyssop received a letter. It was from a certain Alvin Bigshot, manager of a posh seaside hotel which appeared to be suffering from a couple of small but unpleasant problems; problems that could only be explained as ghostly. Mr Bigshot was therefore asking the experts at Hyssop and Co. for immediate – and above all discreet – help.

'Oh, yet another boring old routine job!' Hetty Hyssop sighed. 'But a seaside hotel doesn't sound too bad. It's always nice to have a weekend by the sea.'

Unfortunately in this case she was hugely mistaken.

Hetty Hyssop passed on the news to her assistants, Tom and Hugo the ASG, packed her basic ghosthunting

1

gear, and met the pair of them on Saturday on the train to Bumblebeach.

As I said before, it all started off quite harmlessly.

Hetty Hyssop had reserved an entire compartment on account of Hugo. After all, not everyone can cope with a train journey spent face to face with an ASG, even though these ghosts *are* among the most harmless of their type. Once in the compartment, Tom immediately shut all the curtains: ASGs, like most ghosts, can't stand bright daylight.

'You can come out, Hugo,' he said, dumping his rucksack on the seat.

'Oooooww! Be a bit more careful, please!' came the muffled grumble as Hugo, the third member of the famous ghosthunting trio, wobbled out of the rucksack.

'Cor bloimey,' he moaned. 'Oi hate travelling. Dreadful business!'

'My dear Hugo,' said Hetty Hyssop as she lifted her suitcase on to the luggage rack and put her Thermos of tea on to the foldaway table at her side. 'You certainly didn't have to come. I told you that already. Your help is definitely not necessary in this case. And I'm

quite sure you don't want to spend your time sunbathing on the beach, do you?'

'Very fuuuuunny!' Hugo turned his blueish sulky colour and disappeared up on to the luggage rack.

'I told him we didn't need him too,' said Tom,

plonking himself down on the seat. 'But he was dead set on coming.'

'Typical,' said Hetty Hyssop. 'All ASGs are unbearably nosy!'

She took two red plastic mugs out of her handbag, and handed Tom a packet of sugar lumps and a crumpled letter. 'There you go, young friend,' she said, pouring the tea.

Curious, Hugo leaned down from the parcel rack.

'Take your stinky feet off my head,' growled Tom, trying to make out in the dim light what the letter said. The ASG tickled Tom's neck with icy fingers.

'Hugo, for heaven's sake, stop it!' cried Tom. Irritated, he took off his glasses and cleaned them. 'Push off! Your stupid mouldy breath's steaming up my glasses!'

'Mouldy breath? Mouldy breath?' Hugo wobbled up to the ceiling, looking deeply offended. 'Your rotten tea's to blame!'

Tom just shook his head, put his glasses back on, and read aloud: '"Dear Mr Hyssop."' He raised his head. 'Why "Mr"?'

'Well, that's typical too!' Hetty Hyssop replied. 'People think of a professional ghosthunter, and they imagine a man. Stupid, but very common – unfortunately!'

'"Dear Mr Hyssop,"' Tom read again, '"for some days now, peculiar things have been going on in our hotel – things that, I'm sorry to say, can't be explained by common sense. Hot water has come out of the taps quite abruptly and our air-conditioning system is behaving more and more erratically. Moreover, the most annoying and unpleasant noises can be heard at night, and some of my staff have observed some rather strange things. Since you have an excellent reputation, and are obviously the most renowned expert in the field of ghosthunting, I should like to ask you to free us from these tiresome disturbances. However, I do have to consider the good name of our hotel, so I must ask you for the utmost discretion. With best wishes, Alvin Bigshot."'

'Sounds like a small Fire Ghost!' Tom dropped four lumps of sugar into his mug. 'Just a couple of hours' work, I'd say.'

'Exactly my opinion,' said Hetty Hyssop. 'Which means we'll be able to spend a couple of pleasant hours on the beach. How do you like that idea? Meanwhile our dear friend Hugo can stay safely in the hotel cellar!'

'Very noiice!' groused Hugo from the ceiling. 'Those Foire Ghosts are ridiculous idiots. Oi'd–'

'Quiet!' hissed Hetty Hyssop. Steps could be heard coming along the corridor. The compartment door opened and the ticket collector stuck his head through the curtains.

'Tickets, please!'

Hetty Hyssop passed him the tickets with a friendly smile. Tom cast a worried look at the ceiling, but Hugo had disappeared behind the suitcase.

The ticket collector stamped and returned the tickets to Hetty Hyssop with a nod. But just as he was about to leave the compartment something grabbed his cap. Something wobbly, cold and mouldy green. Horrified, he looked up – where his cap was floating ten centimetres above his head and, above the cap, a ghost with flapping hair and garish green eyes was grinning down at him maliciously.

'Hellooooooo!' Hugo purred. Then he dropped the cap back on the ticket collector's head, blew his cold and stinky breath into the poor man's face, and disappeared back into the rucksack.

'Hugo!' cried Tom angrily.

The ticket collector stood there trembling, his teeth chattering so loudly that the people in the next compartment could hear them.

'Is there something wrong with the tickets, sir?' asked Hetty Hyssop in her deep, reassuring voice.

The poor ticket collector couldn't stop trembling. He cast a fearful look around the whole compartment, but there wasn't the teeny-weeniest bit of mouldy green anywhere to be seen.

'Are you looking for something?' Tom tried to sound as innocent as possible.

The ticket collector wiped his brow and murmured, 'Next stop: Bumblebeach!' Then he stumbled out of the compartment as fast as his short legs could carry him, and slammed the door behind him.

'Oh, that silly ASG!' groaned Hetty Hyssop. 'Hugo, have you lost what's left of your ghostly mind? This isn't a pleasure trip!'

'Don't you go showing yourself so quickly again!' Tom called up to the luggage rack. 'You're nothing but trouble!'

'Yooooou don't let a poor ghost do anything!'

came an offended voice from the rucksack. 'Yooooou don't know how to have fun! No fun at all!'

Hetty Hyssop just shook her head. 'That's what comes of travelling with a ghost. I dare say our own ASG will give us more bother than Mr Bigshot's Fire Ghost!'

Unfortunately, she was badly mistaken once again. But how was Hetty Hyssop supposed to know that Mr Bigshot had concealed various important things from her, and that she and Tom would soon need Hugo's help rather urgently?

Damaged by a Ghost

Hyssop and Co. took a taxi to the hotel. Hugo hid himself in Tom's rucksack again and, thankfully, stayed there. Only once did his long white arm come floating out to pinch the taxi driver's ear. Naturally, though, Tom was the prime suspect.

The Seafront Hotel was indeed right on the seafront. A large and beautiful park separated it from the coastal road, and if you went down a couple of wooden steps from the rear veranda, you came out on to a private beach full of signs saying SEAFRONT HOTEL GUESTS ONLY.

Tom had never been in a hotel before, never mind a hotel like this. The only thing that marred the idyllic impression of the place was a big black mark on the roof. Hetty Hyssop didn't like the look of that at all.

'Strange!' she murmured. 'Very strange indeed!'

The taxi deposited them by the Seafront's main entrance, and a bellboy immediately came running

10

down the immense flight of steps to carry their bags –
an offer which Hetty Hyssop refused with a smile.

'Wow, this is some pile!' said Tom as they climbed
the steps.

'Oi want to see it too,' grumbled Hugo from within
the rucksack.

'You stay in there for now,' hissed Hetty Hyssop.
'Your little joke on the train was quite enough. In any
case, it's much too light!'

She and Tom passed through the elegant entrance hall and made for the reception desk. A couple of guests were sitting in front of a huge fireplace, but nobody seemed to take much notice of the two ghosthunters.

'Not doing bad business, considering it's not peak holiday time,' observed Tom.

He looked around curiously. A short fat man was standing behind the reception desk, sorting the post into the guests' pigeonholes.

'Good morning,' said Hetty Hyssop with a friendly smile, putting her business card down on the counter. 'Would you mind telling Mr Bigshot that we're here?'

The little man glanced at the business card, gave a start, and dropped all his letters.

Evidently damaged by a ghost, thought Tom. He had come to recognise the signs immediately: pasty skin, trembling earlobes, chewed bottom lip and – quite typical for a place haunted by Fire Ghosts – a faint, barely noticeable smell of burning about his hair and clothes.

'Ju – just a moment, please!' The head receptionist shot off, whereupon the ghosthunters took the opportunity to have an innocent look around the hall.

'Except for the staff's symptoms, there's no trace of anything,' whispered Hetty.

'Not even any ashes,' Tom whispered back. 'And none of the plug sockets are black, either!'

'Dead right!' Hetty Hyssop nodded. 'Everything's pointing to a harmless attack!'

Before they could make any further observations, the head receptionist returned with the manager in tow. Alvin Bigshot was a large bald man with a small, perfectly groomed moustache, a white suit, and shoes so highly polished you could see your reflection in them. The sight of Hetty Hyssop and Tom seemed to come as quite a surprise to him.

'Hyssop and Co.?' he asked. 'The . . .' He looked around hastily and lowered his voice. 'The ghosthunters?'

'Mr Bigshot, I presume?' Hetty shook his hand firmly. 'I suggest we don't stand around here, but go and talk in your office. What do you think?'

The manager nodded uncertainly and showed them into a smartly furnished office with a massive desk harbouring four telephones and a small aquarium crowded with tiny fish.

'Please, do take a seat, Hetty, erm . . .'

'Hyssop,' said Hetty, relieving herself of her suitcase and sitting down. 'I presume you're looking so

13

confused because I'm a woman, not to mention quite an *old* woman? That's stupid, you know, so forget it!'

The manager opened and shut his mouth like one of his fish.

'Here on my right,' continued Hetty Hyssop, 'is my assistant, Tom. Don't be deceived by his age: he's a highly experienced ghosthunter. I'll introduce my other helper to you once the curtains are shut. Would you mind . . .?'

'Er, yes, of course!' The manager sprang up and drew the curtains.

'Green,' Tom observed with a frown. 'Are all the hotel curtains green?'

The manager nodded.

Tom shrugged his shoulders. 'Not the most favourable colour when it comes to ghosts,' he said. 'You should think yourself lucky that we're dealing with Fire Ghosts here!'

'Really? Erm, why's that?' asked Mr Bigshot, tugging nervously at his moustache.

'Fire Ghosts like all colours,' explained Tom. 'Most other ghosts, though, are particularly keen on green. They hate red, but they're attracted to green, especially mouldy green!'

The manager looked anxiously at his curtains.

'You'll see for yourself any moment,' said Hetty Hyssop. 'Hugo, you can come out now. But be careful not to slime on everything, OK?'

'Oh, at last!' groaned the ASG, wobbling out of Tom's rucksack pale as a mushroom and large as life. 'Oh, woooonderful!' he sighed, looking around. 'Everything's green!'

Mr Bigshot gave a sharp cry of horror and disappeared under his desk.

Tom grinned, and Hugo doubled in size with pride.

'Honestly, Mr Bigshot! What's all the fuss about?' Hetty Hyssop rapped on his desk. 'Come on out, there's nothing to worry about. This is my other assistant, Hugo the ASG!'

'But . . . but . . .' Mr Bigshot's voice trembled. 'But it's a ghost!'

'Absolutely right,' replied Hetty Hyssop. 'Could we please get on with discussing our assignment now?'

Hesitantly, the manager crept out from under his desk. Beads of sweat glistened on his bald patch, and his moustache looked positively dishevelled. 'I'm sorry,

I'm just n – n – not used to seeing such things!' he stammered, sitting down on his chair again.

'No worries,' breathed Hugo, offering Mr Bigshot his white hand.

As ASG fingers are icy cold, the manager gave a start when he shook it. And as they are always pretty slimy, Alvin Bigshot hastily wiped his hand on a tissue before he addressed Hetty Hyssop again.

'Mr, erm, Hugo,' he said, clearing his throat, 'doesn't look like our ghost so far as I know. I've never actually seen it myself, but the porter and a bellboy said they saw something transparent that was small and reddish and stank of sulphur. I personally . . .' he nervously tugged at his moustache again, 'I personally didn't believe a word of it, to be honest, because . . .' He gave Hugo a sheepish look. 'I – don't take it the wrong way – I don't actually believe in ghosts. But then there was all the business with the hot water and, er, the steam from the air conditioning, and this faint burning smell everywhere without there being a fire. Highly unpleasant!' The manager cleared his throat again. 'This is a luxury hotel, if you get my drift, and the whole thing has to be handled very discreetly. After all, we've got a reputation to protect. A nice relaxing

place to unwind and all that sort of thing, if you see what I mean.'

Hetty Hyssop nodded. 'Are these apparitions especially bad in any particular part of the hotel?'

The manager cleared his throat yet again. 'On the fourth floor. Things on the fourth floor are . . . somewhat problematic!'

'What's that supposed to mean?' Tom asked suspiciously. He had a sneaking feeling that Mr Bigshot wasn't telling them everything he knew.

'Well, er . . .' The manager tapped a golden fountain pen nervously against his desk. 'I'm not quite up to speed with the current state of play, but . . .'

'And what exactly is *that* supposed to mean?' asked Hetty Hyssop, rubbing her pointy nose. She, too, was gradually losing patience.

The second telephone on the left rang. 'No calls!' Alvin Bigshot snapped into it, and slammed the receiver down.

Hetty Hyssop repeated her question. 'Once again – what do you mean, you're "not quite up to speed with the current state of play"?'

'Since yesterday, the staff have been refusing to go up to the fourth floor,' muttered Alvin Bigshot. 'But, I mean, bellboys and chambermaids are always scaredy-cats, aren't they?'

'What about the guests?' asked Tom.

The manager shrugged his shoulders. 'They . . . well . . .' He wiped his hand across his sweaty bald patch. 'They didn't come down for breakfast. But come on, that doesn't necessarily mean anything. All these daft rumours about ghosts will just have made them,

you know, feel a bit intimidated. It's all a storm in a teacup, if you ask me!'

Tom and Hetty Hyssop exchanged alarmed looks, and Hugo collapsed down to half his size.

'Oooooooooh, that doesn't sound good,' he moaned. 'Not good at all. No!'

Hetty Hyssop stood up abruptly. 'I'm most annoyed, Mr Bigshot. Extremely annoyed!'

The manager slumped down. 'Well, I thought, there's no point making things sound worse than they are. Do you see what I mean? All the hoo-ha, the guests . . .'

'My dear sir, you just don't understand!' Hetty Hyssop thumped the desk. 'Thanks to your earlier mis-information, we haven't brought the right equipment! So I can only hope that we really are just dealing with a small problem here!' She turned to Tom. 'What do you think? We could still risk an initial fact-finding mis-sion, couldn't we?'

'Of course!' said Tom, although he wasn't entirely comfortable with the idea.

'Hugo?'

'That shoooould be enough. Foire Ghosts are as thick as two short planks.'

'Right, then!' Hetty Hyssop picked up her suitcase. 'Let's go and have a look at the fourth floor. Where can we get changed?'

Alvin Bigshot quickly sprang up. 'Please, be my guests. Along here!' He led the three ghosthunters into a small side room and, bowing profusely, left them alone.

'Well, then!' With a sigh Hetty Hyssop opened her suitcase. 'To work, my men. Let's hope it's no harder than we thought it would be!'

The First Fiery Encounter

When the three ghosthunters returned to Mr Bigshot's office, they looked rather strange.

All three were wearing firemen's helmets and flying goggles. Hugo's goggles were tinted to protect him from daylight. Hetty Hyssop and Tom were wearing special suits made of heat-resistant foil, which they had smeared with a special paste consisting of SPF 30 sunscreen and sugared olive oil. This paste was, admittedly, somewhat sticky, but extremely useful in an encounter with a Fire Ghost.

In addition, Hetty Hyssop had a baking tray on her back and, attached to her belt, a mini vacuum cleaner, a bag of sugar lumps, oven gloves and a device that looked like an enormous hairdryer.

Tom was carrying his rucksack, which contained cake icing and several other useful things. In his right hand, he held an icing baster with a particularly large nozzle. It was filled with red cake icing.

Finally, Hugo, who like all ASGs detested heat, had covered himself in a bag made of heat-resistant foil. The only things left poking out were his head in its helmet, his wobbly fingers, and his feet – which were covered by special shoes just like Hetty Hyssop's and Tom's. This had one great advantage: it stopped Hugo from leaving behind his slimy trails, which could be quite a danger for his ghosthunting colleagues, since they could easily get stuck in the slime at the most precarious moments.

Alvin Bigshot stared at the three ghosthunters as if they'd appeared from another planet.

'You must have a lift,' said Hetty Hyssop. 'Could you please show us the way?'

The manager still stared at them, quite transfixed, but finally he pulled himself together and hurried to the office door.

'The service lift,' he said. 'The best thing to do is to take the goods lift from the kitchen – because of the guests, if you get my drift!'

Hastily he led the ghosthunters down a long corridor. Delicious smells wafted towards them, and Tom realised that he was hungry.

'Hugo, you'd better get into that rucksack!' he hissed to the ghost.

'Yeah, yeah, all right!' grumbled Hugo, disappearing just in time, for Alvin Bigshot was already opening the door to the massive hotel kitchens.

As soon as the ghosthunters walked through the door, the chefs and trainees alike dropped all sorts of things into their cooking pots that didn't belong there. (Several guests would later complain that the chicken soup tasted of raspberry and the chocolate pudding of fish.) And when Hugo's white hand waved from Tom's rucksack, two head chefs (identifiable by their large hats) fainted on the spot. One took three saucepans with him, the contents of which splashed all over his spotless white overalls.

'No cause for alarm, staff!' cried Mr Bigshot. 'These are just three well-respected ghosthunters who have come to sort out our little problem on the fourth floor!'

His words didn't have much effect. On the contrary, the chefs turned as white as their hats.

'Ghosthunters, sir?' asked the fattest of them. 'G – g – ghosts?'

'Precisely,' said Tom. 'So if you wouldn't mind, where is this goods lift? We haven't got all day!'

'Along here!' Alvin Bigshot cleared a path through the chefs, who were still standing there like waxwork dummies.

At that very moment, it happened. With a loud bang, an oven door burst open and something bright red and repellently stinky flew out with a terrible scream. The clothes and hats of five chefs turned to ashes on the spot, leaving the poor chaps standing there clad in nothing but their underwear. One of them, totally baffled, was holding a burning spoon in his hand.

Tom immediately pulled out the icing baster, but the chefs – now hopping, wailing and running wildly all over the place – blocked his view. However he craned and strained, the Fire Ghost was simply nowhere to be seen.

'What's the matter?' Tom heard Hugo asking from within the rucksack. 'What's all that noise about?'

'There, Tom!' cried Hetty Hyssop, shoving two chefs aside. 'There, in front of you!'

Like a firework, the flickering ghost whizzed away over their heads. Tom felt unpleasantly warm even under his helmet.

'No water!' cried Hetty Hyssop, but it was already too late. One chef raised his arm and chucked a whole bucket of water at the ghost. Hissing, the water evaporated as it hit the wobbling red body. The Fire Ghost

licked its flickering lips and sizzled right up to the ceiling. Soot tumbled blackly down on to the hats and into the soup, which the guests would later find revoltingly crunchy. Horrified, the chefs stumbled against one another, but Tom and Hetty Hyssop finally saw their chance.

'Eeeeeeaaaargh!' screeched the fiery creature, blowing its hot breath at them – but Hetty Hyssop's splendid special paste reduced it to room temperature. All Tom could feel was a pleasantly tickling sensation on his skin.

'Come and get it!' he cried, and squirted so much icing at the ghost's chest that it looked like a wedding cake. Hetty Hyssop leaped to Tom's side and switched on her mini vacuum cleaner.

The sugared Fire Ghost desperately tried to fly off, but the cake icing made it heavy and slow, and it became thinner and thinner as it was drawn towards Hetty Hyssop's vacuum cleaner. With one last desperate effort it tried to hide under an extractor hood but Tom, quick as a flash, pulled on an oven glove, grabbed the ghost – which was as thin as a shoelace by now – and stuffed it into a Thermos flask.

'Hurrah!' cried the chefs, throwing their hats in the

air – with one, unfortunately, landing in the tomato soup. A relieved smile appeared under Alvin Bigshot's moustache.

'Well, that must have been it,' said Hetty Hyssop. 'Looks as if we're spared a trip to the fourth floor!'

But Tom nudged her and pointed to a plug socket.

'I don't believe it!' he whispered. 'Look!'

Sparks were darting out of the plug holes, followed by little clouds of vile violet smoke. The two ghosthunters exchanged worried looks.

'What, erm, what does that mean?' Alvin Bigshot asked nervously.

'That means we'll have to go to the fourth floor after all!' replied Tom. His tummy suddenly gave a peculiar lurch. 'There!' he said, pressing the Fire Ghost-filled Thermos flask into the baffled manager's hand. 'Don't open it, whatever you do. Now, where's that goods lift, then?'

Attack in the Elevator

'I suggest we only go as far as the third floor!' said Hetty Hyssop when the lift door closed behind them. 'And then we'll creep up the stairs. OK?'

Tom nodded and pressed the button.

'Can oi finally come out?' grumbled Hugo, wobbling out of the rucksack. He looked around, astonished. 'What's all this?' With a jolt, the lift started moving, and Hugo was jerked against the wall.

'Help!' he wailed. 'Help! What's going on?'

Tom giggled. 'It's a lift, you dumbo!'

'Oh, really?' Irritated, Hugo blew his mouldy breath into Tom's face. 'And what use is that to anyone?'

'Ssh! Just be quiet!' Hetty Hyssop looked anxiously at her feet. 'Do you notice anything?'

Tom looked down. He could feel something warm, very warm, beneath the soles of his shoes. Fortunately his shoes, like Hetty Hyssop's, were filled with aluminium foil folded thirteen times over, and had specially coated soles.

'What's that?' he whispered.

The floor of the lift turned bright red and bubbles started to form. 'Oi'm suffocating!' wailed Hugo, and floated up to the ceiling.

But it was no cooler there either.

'Watch out!' cried Hetty Hyssop, and she and Tom clung to one another. The lift went faster and faster, as if someone were shoving it along from below.

Any second now, we'll go through the roof, thought Tom. He squeezed his eyes tightly shut, but that made it even worse. So he opened them again – only to see a fiery finger boring a hole through the red-hot floor. Tom jumped back with a yell.

Another finger appeared, and another, and another, until an entire hand was poking up through the floor, fiery red and steaming. *Snap!* It made a grab for Tom's legs.

Hugo was hanging beneath the ceiling, howling like a dog. Hetty Hyssop, however, sprang protectively in front of Tom, who was trembling and kicking wildly, and threw sugar lumps all over the fiery hand. Like

frightened worms, the fingers jerked back and disappeared into the floor, hissing as they went.

The lift raced on, braked sharply, plunged back
down, whistling as it went, and rattled up again. The

ghosthunters desperately tried to stay on their feet. Tom kept bashing the emergency brake, but nothing happened. Then, with a terrible jolt which almost threw them on to the red-hot floor, the lift finally stopped. Groaning, it hung on its cables.

'What – what's wrong now?' whispered Tom. He got the answer at once.

With a hiss the lift door opened and a truly repulsive fiery-red head with eyes like light bulbs grinned at them. It opened its massive mouth, and yellow ghostly flames licked Tom's legs.

'The icing!' cried Hetty. 'Go on, Tom!'

His fingers trembling, Tom shot the rest of the icing into the fiery mouth.

The grisly creature clearly didn't like the taste. It had a terrible attack of hiccups that shook the lift as if it were a baby's rattle. Hetty Hyssop grabbed the baking tray from her back and banged it hard on the gruesome ghost's head. With a belch, the head disappeared into thin air.

The door banged shut, and the lift hung clanking and groaning in the air somewhere between the floors.

'It's turning cooler again!' whispered Tom. He was still trembling slightly. His icing baster was empty;

Hetty Hyssop's baking tray lay on the ground, dented beyond repair.

'Hell's bells, that certainly wasn't any normal Foire Ghost!' grumbled Hugo, floating gently to the ground.

'No, it certainly wasn't!' Hetty Hyssop tried to fix her baking tray on to her back again. She looked very irritated. 'That Bigshot played the problem down so much that we almost ended up as joss sticks. He's in for it – *if* we ever get out of here in one piece!' The tip of her nose was positively hot with rage. 'What do you reckon, Tom? Should we go up or down?'

'Up,' he replied.

'Up? What do yooooooou mean, up?' Hugo waggled his icy fingers around indignantly under Tom's nose. 'Doesn't anyone care what *oi* think?'

'Nah,' said Tom. 'In any case, you run off and hide the moment things get a bit tricky!'

'Fine. *Fiiiine*. If that's how yoooou want things!' Hugo folded his white arms across his chest. 'Then yoooou can save yooooourselves from this thing. Oi'm not helping yoooou! No, oi have my pride tooooooo!' And with that, he disappeared into Tom's rucksack.

'Pass me the spare icing baster,' demanded Tom.

Hugo's white hand emerged, and threw the baster

at Tom's head. Tom just grinned and pressed the button for the third floor once more. The lift set off again with a jolt, and rattled as it flew upwards.

'My dear Tom,' said Hetty Hyssop. 'You really are a remarkably brave young man. I simply couldn't have a better assistant!'

'Oh, it's nothing!' murmured Tom, straightening his glasses in embarrassment.

Then the lift stopped.

But not on the third floor.

It stopped on the fourth.

The Fourth Floor

The lift door opened with a faint squeak. Thick clouds of violet smoke wafted in. They stank. A stink that somehow managed to be simultaneously sweet and burny. It made Tom cough.

'Clips on!' said Hetty Hyssop.

'There yoooooou go!' Hugo passed two nose clips out from the rucksack, and poked his own nose out. He sniffed around. 'Oi don't know what your problem is. It smells delicious, absolutely delicious!'

'To ghosts, maybe,' said Tom. 'But it smells pretty nasty to me!' The nose clip made his voice sound funny, though Hetty Hyssop didn't sound any better.

'Look at that!' she said through her nose.

Tom cautiously stuck his head out of the door. The violet smoke was making his eyes burn and water. But what he could make out was rather disturbing. The lift was situated at the end of a long corridor with count-less bedroom doors. The cream carpet was disfigured by a trail of burned-in footprints, all of them worry-ingly large. But what was even more worrying was this: huge flames were leaping out of the walls and doors. They crackled and stank, and bathed the corridor in a reddish-violet light. The only window at the end of the corridor was completely covered in soot. The wall lamps between the bedroom doors had melted, as had the brass room numbers.

'My dear Tom, I fear the worst,' muttered Hetty.

'A Category Three Fire Ghost?' whispered Tom.

'At the very least!' Hetty whispered back. 'In fact, I fear something quite different. All this looks suspiciously like a – no! We can't even think of it!'

Tom looked at her, disturbed – but Hetty Hyssop gave him no time to think about what she'd said. She stepped boldly out into the burning corridor and walked right through the midst of the flames.

'Come on, young man!' she cried. 'It's just ghost-fire. No problem for our specially pasted suits!'

With trembling fingers, Tom set his glasses straight and followed her. She was right. The flames engulfed him, reaching right above his head and dropping down on to his helmet; but the only thing he felt was a faint tingling on his skin, slightly unpleasant but perfectly bearable. Tom looked around. All the bedroom doors were shut, their locks all hot and bent. He could feel Hugo rummaging around in the rucksack. That pesky ASG was just too nosy to stay hidden the whole time. Eventually he peeped over Tom's shoulder.

'Nice work!' he commented.

'Yuk!' whispered Tom. 'Do you have to keep

blowing your breath right in my face? It's stinky enough in here as it is!'

'With that stupid clip on your nose, yoooooou can't smell anything anyway,' breathed Hugo. 'Know what? Yoooooou sound like a duck!' His hollow laugh sounded very spooky echoing through the burning corridor.

'Hugo!' hissed Hetty Hyssop. 'Come on, make yourself useful. Float through the bedroom doors and see if you can dig up any guests!'

'What? Me?' Hugo immediately disappeared behind Tom's shoulder. 'Through there? Oi'd evaporate most miserably!'

'Oh, come off it!' Hetty Hyssop put her hands on her hips. 'You're a ghost. This dreadful heat can't do you any harm at all. Especially not with that bag you're wearing. So off you go!'

Grumbling, Hugo floated across the corridor and disappeared through the first closed door.

'Nothing!' he declared when he re-emerged. 'It's all pretty chaotic in there, but no guests!'

Hugo floated into each room in turn, only to find the same thing every time. All the guests had vanished without trace. Hetty Hyssop's expression became ever darker.

'This just confirms my worst fears,' she murmured when in the last room Hugo once again failed to find anyone. 'My very worst fears of all. Tom, stay clear of the sockets!'

'Wh – wh – why?' stammered Tom. His courage was gradually ebbing away from him after all.

'I'll be able to explain better once we're back downstairs,' said Hetty Hyssop. 'Come on, let's beat it. But we'll use the stairs this time!'

They had almost reached the stairs when all of a sudden they heard a knocking. They looked around, shocked.

'It came from that cupboard over there!' whispered Tom. He pointed to one of the linen cupboards right next to the lift. Cautiously they crept back. The knocking came again.

Holding the mini vacuum cleaner in her hand, Hetty Hyssop wrenched the cupboard door open with a jolt.

In a corner, between the duvet covers and piles of hand towels, cowered a small bellboy. He was trembling so much that the metal buttons on his uniform clattered together like castanets.

'Good heavens!' Hetty Hyssop carefully pulled the little chap out of the mountains of linen. He was as skinny as a stick insect. 'How long have you been in there? You must feel like the Sunday roast!'

The bellboy managed a tiny and desperate smile, but could not utter a word through his trembling lips. He wouldn't have been able to stay upright without the two ghosthunters' help.

'Ha-haaaa! Something's certainly given him a good fright!' Hugo grinned mischievously and shoved him in the chest. The bellboy gave a sharp scream and immediately made for the cupboard again – but Tom and Hetty Hyssop held on to him.

'Don't worry!' said Tom. 'That's Hugo. He just acts horrible. He's totally harmless!'

'What?' Hugo inflated himself – not without difficulty, given that he was clad in a foil bag. 'Harmless? Did yooooou call me harmless?'

'Put a sock in it, Hugo!' said Hetty Hyssop crossly. 'You're to carry this poor boy here to the stairs. And woe betide you if you frighten him again. Got it?'

'Yeah, yeah, I get all the toughest jobs!' moaned Hugo. All the same, though, he took the bellboy on his back. By now the boy had ceased to care what happened to him anyway. Only when he touched Hugo's icy back did he flinch for a moment.

'Off we go, then!' whispered Hetty Hyssop. 'Let's get out of here!'

They ran along the burning corridor, looking back with ever increasing anxiety.

'Hetty!' whispered Tom. 'I've got a very strange feeling!'

Hetty Hyssop stopped and listened. 'A shower!' she whispered.

Now Tom could hear it too: a splashing and running of water, interspersed with contented grunts and snuffles. It sounded horrible.

'Wh – wh – wh – what – what's h – h – h – having a sh – sh – shower?' stammered Tom. 'Th – th – the–' A terrific bang stopped him mid-sentence.

Behind them, all hell was breaking loose. Sparks, flashes, and balls of fire as big as children's heads were shooting out of the walls and ceiling. 'Run!' cried Hetty. The stairs were still five bedroom doors away.

'Aaaaaaaaaaaaaaarrrrrrrrrggggghhh!' moaned something behind them, sounding so hideous that Tom's legs turned to jelly and Hugo turned pink all over.

'Come on, down the stairs!' Hetty Hyssop pulled from her belt the strange hairdryer-like thing, and switched it on. It sounded like a police siren, and puffed icy-cold air into the path of the thing that was coming at them from the flames.

Flickering, it stopped.

Hugo and Tom stumbled down the first few steps while Hetty Hyssop was still standing on the landing. Tom turned to her, worried, and finally got a really good look at the ghost which had been following them. It looked like a walking fire.

The icy air from Hetty Hyssop's fan did prevent it from coming any closer, but it didn't seem to bother it particularly. The ghost twisted its hideous face into a grin, pressed its fiery fists against the walls and opened its cavernous jaws. A hot puff of air swept thunderously towards Hetty Hyssop, and blew her and her two assistants down the stairs. They tumbled down a whole floor before they could get back on their feet – and there was the fiery monster still laughing at them, its laugh hollow, hideous and abysmally mean.

Bad, Bad, Bad

etty Hyssop marched straight across the hotel's entrance hall, her white curls flapping and her face covered in soot. Tom and Hugo, with the bellboy on his back, could barely keep up with her.

The guests, who were reading their papers in front of the fireplace, spilled their coffee into their laps with shock when they saw the ghosthunters. Hugo's white figure in particular provoked piercing squeals and a couple of faintings. The ASG, of course, was delighted. And Hetty Hyssop didn't care. She was boiling with rage; frothing with rage; really fit to burst with rage.

Without a word she handed the bellboy, who was still shaking slightly, to the astonished porter. Then she stormed into Alvin Bigshot's office, Tom and Hugo trailing in her wake.

The manager was standing behind his desk, feeding the fish. He dropped the tub into the aquarium when Hetty Hyssop wrenched open the door.

'What, what . . . er, what's the matter?' he asked, baffled.

'Come with us!' said Hetty Hyssop, taking him by the tie and dragging him to the door.

'But my dear Mrs Hyssop!' protested Alvin Bigshot, trying in vain to escape. 'Whatever has happened? Have – have you solved our little problem?'

'Our little problem!' The tip of Hetty Hyssop's nose began to twitch. 'I don't know whether you're simply stupid or a confirmed liar. Whatever the case, I need fresh air, or I'll explode!'

She dragged the manager, who was by now poppy red with embarrassment, through the dining room, past his guests who were eating their meals, out on to the large veranda and then down the steps to the beach. Only there did she stop on the soft sand, and release his tie.

With trembling fingers Alvin Bigshot straightened it, and looked around uncomfortably. The beach was empty save for a couple of walkers in the distance. The sky was grey and the sea wind blew fine drizzle into their faces. Even Hugo found this wonderful after the oven-like fourth floor. But Alvin Bigshot looked most unhappy.

'I don't understand, madam!' he complained, buttoning up his white suit. 'Why don't we go inside and have a little something to eat? We'll catch a chill out here!'

'Don't you "Madam" me!' said Hetty Hyssop, taking off her aluminium shoes. 'We're going for a walk along the beach now, and you can finally tell me what's *really* been going on here recently.'

'Oi'd loike a little nap.' Hugo yawned and disappeared into the rucksack, before Tom also took off his shoes and tramped along behind Hetty Hyssop and the hotel manager. The soles of his feet were still quite hot from their fiery adventure, and the cool sand felt good on them. Even the cold autumn wind was pleasantly refreshing after the heat on the fourth floor. Though Tom could certainly have done with something to eat.

'Hot water!' spluttered Hetty Hyssop. 'Broken air conditioning! Thanks to you and your barefaced half-truths, we could have been burned to a cinder up there! And that bellboy we found in the linen cupboard – didn't you notice he was missing?'

'A bellboy?' The manager shook the sand from his shoes. 'Well, you know, we have so many of them. You don't tend to notice if you're one short!'

This rendered Hetty Hyssop almost speechless.

'Do you know what we should do with you?' she asked in a threateningly calm voice.

The manager twirled his moustache nervously.

'I know,' said Tom. 'We should put him in the

goods lift and send him up to the fourth floor. Then he can take a closer look at his "little problem"!'

Alvin Bigshot threw an evil glance at Tom. 'A tasteless suggestion!' he said. 'Truly tasteless!'

'Oh, I don't think it's at all bad,' said Hetty Hyssop. 'And I'll ask Hugo to make it happen if you don't finally tell me the whole story. About the thunderstorm, for starters!'

Tom looked at her in amazement. Alvin Bigshot, however, turned as pale as Hugo's ghostly chest.

'How do you know about that?' he gasped.

'Why didn't you tell me?' asked Hetty Hyssop, sinking down into a deckchair.

'Well, you know . . .' Alvin Bigshot cleared his throat and looked down at his once so carefully polished shoes, which now were full of sand. 'It mustn't get around that we have, erm, such violent thunderstorms here. Unfortunately they happen quite a lot and, um, some guests find storms like that extremely off-putting. You get my drift. At the end of the day, we use our good climate in our advertising. Sea air is healthy throughout the year and so on. You know the sort of thing. And quite apart from that,' the manager nervously ran a hand across his bald patch, which was already quite wet from the rain, 'quite apart from that, there's no way I could have known that storms would be of any interest to you!' He sneezed. 'See? Now I've caught a chill!'

Hetty Hyssop dug her toes into the sand, looking gloomy. 'OK. You couldn't know anything about the significance of storms when you're plagued by ghosts, and I,' she sighed, 'I should have asked you. But when you made it all sound so harmless, it never occurred to me that we might be dealing with something so incredibly dangerous!'

'Incredibly dangerous?' repeated the manager. 'Dangerous? What do you mean?'

Tom swallowed and remembered the sight of the Fire Ghost blowing them down the stairs.

'Did your lightning conductor work when the last storm hit you?' asked Hetty Hyssop.

'Not really,' admitted Alvin Bigshot. 'Could we go inside now, please?' He sneezed again.

'My goodness, surely you can stand a bit of sea air!' Hetty Hyssop snapped impatiently.

'I hate the sea,' muttered the manager, looking at the grey waves with distaste.

'What do you mean, your lightning conductor

"didn't really work"?' asked Tom. 'Did it work, or didn't it?'

'All your telephones suddenly went dead,' said Hetty Hyssop. 'Didn't they, Bigshot?'

The manager looked at her in astonishment. 'And how do you know *that*?'

'So it's true! That's a catastrophe!' Hetty Hyssop tore at her white curls. 'That means we're dealing with one of the five most dangerous ghosts on earth – and what kind of equipment have we got? Children's toys, nothing but children's toys. My sole consolation is that hardly anything works against this monster anyway!'

Alvin Bigshot looked at her in horror.

And Tom suddenly felt sick. 'So what kind of ghost is it?' he asked.

Hetty Hyssop hauled herself up from the deckchair with a deep sigh. 'It's a GILIG. No doubt about it. I've never come across this kind of ghost in my entire career, and goodness knows I could have done without it now!'

'A what?' stammered the ashen-faced manager.

Tom just stood there staring at the hotel. It looked spooky, he thought. He could make out something flickering red through the soot-stained windows.

'A GILIG!' he whispered. 'Oh no!'

'But what *is* that?' cried Alvin Bigshot in despair. 'Just tell me!'

'Tom, you explain,' said Hetty Hyssop and, taking one last look at the sea, she tramped back to the hotel. Tom followed her, Alvin Bigshot trailing by his side, nervously trying to catch his eye.

'So, what is it?' he asked once again in a shaky voice.

Tom knew only too well what a GILIG was. He had studied every volume of Hetty Hyssop's ghost encyclopaedia in great depth. There was something about GILIGs in Volume 23. *Particularly disgusting apparitions*, it said. The article could be summarised in very few words: the chances of surviving an encounter with this ghost were pretty much zilch.

What Now?

'GILIG stands for Gruesome Invincible LIghtning Ghost,' explained Tom as he and Alvin Bigshot made their way up the steps to the hotel veranda. Hugo was still snoring away peacefully in the rucksack. 'GILIGs materialise in the case of particularly violent lightning, and mostly get into buildings down the telephone lines. Once they're in, it's incredibly difficult to get rid of them again without smashing the whole building to smithereens!'

The manager almost pulled off his moustache in shock.

'GILIGs can reduce humans to ashes or shrivel them up,' Tom continued. 'But their favourite thing is to turn them into minor Fire Ghosts!'

'Which is presumably what happened to your fourth-floor guests,' said Hetty Hyssop over her shoulder. 'How many of them were there?'

'Seven.' The manager sighed faintly. He looked completely crushed as they made their way across the formal lounge. Once again, all the guests turned to look at them, but none of the ghosthunters took any notice.

'Seven!' Hetty Hyssop shook her head. 'And that on top of everything else. We've caught one, so that leaves six. Goodness knows where they've got to. Where did you put the Thermos flask?'

'On my desk,' murmured the manager.

'Good,' said Hetty Hyssop. 'Then let's have a closer look at our prisoner!'

The Thermos flask stood next to the aquarium. Hetty Hyssop slipped on an oven glove, carefully opened the lid, and fished out the captured ghost. It looked distinctly pale and dopey, though not as thinly stretched as when Tom had first caught it.

'This flask contains dry ice,' explained Hetty Hyssop. 'It cools Fire Ghosts without bringing them into contact with water. Come closer, Bigshot. Does this ghost look like any of your missing guests?'

Hesitantly, the manager came closer. 'Oh my goodness!' he cried in surprise. 'It's Mrs Elsie Redmond. She's been staying with us for years, always in October.

Incredible!' He moved even closer. 'I have to say, the transformation didn't do her any favours!'

'Tom, dear,' Hetty Hyssop stuffed the fiery Mrs Redmond back into the Thermos flask and screwed the lid on tightly, 'send Mr Lovely a fax and ask him to find my textbooks and copy down all the information he can find about GILIGs, and then fax it back to us. I know dangerously little about these monsters!'

'Done,' said Tom, and rushed to reception, where the hotel fax machine was located. Mr Lovely had been a good friend of Hyssop and Co. ever since the ghost-hunters had saved him from a monstrous IRG (Incredibly Revolting Ghost). In haste, Tom scribbled down Hetty Hyssop's message, handed it to the porter and shot back to the manager's office. When he got there, Hugo had just finished his little nap and was floating up by the ceiling, yawning. The manager was feeding his fish again, and Hetty Hyssop was sitting on the edge of the desk tapping her foot impatiently.

'As soon as Mr Lovely's information arrives,' she said, 'I'll write you out a list of things we'll need before it turns dark. And please let your guests and staff know at once about the dangerous situation. Tom will listen and make sure that you don't play it all down as shamelessly as you have done so far!'

'What?' Mr Bigshot recoiled from the old lady as if she personally were the GILIG. 'What am I supposed to do? Tell the guests? Have you gone mad?' He shook his head energetically. He couldn't *stop* shaking his head. 'No. No. You can't ask me to do that! Over my dead body! I'd be ruined, don't you see? Utterly ruined! No, no, never. *No!*'

'Fine!' Hetty Hyssop shrugged her shoulders. 'As you prefer. In that case Hugo will tell everyone!'

'It'd be my pleasure!' Hugo floated towards the office door, filled with gleeful anticipation. But quick as a flash Alvin Bigshot blocked his way.

'Stop!' he cried. 'Stop. Very well, I'll do it. I call this mean-minded blackmail, but I'll do what you want!'

'You'd better,' said Tom. 'Or do you think your guests will still be able to pay their hotel bills once they've been turned into Fire Ghosts?'

The manager looked at the Thermos flask containing Mrs Redmond, then went slowly back to his desk and lifted the receiver of the telephone on the right.

'Tell the guests to assemble, please,' he said sullenly. 'Yes, of course that means all of them. And all the staff too. Ten minutes in the lounge. I've got an important announcement to make!'

Then he slammed the receiver down and plopped into his armchair.

'You must have all the sockets on the ground floor sealed up with icing,' said Hetty Hyssop. 'Otherwise the GILIG will eavesdrop on us – and we don't want that, do we?'

'Icing!' whispered the manager. 'Sockets. Icing. I think I'm going mad!'

Great Excitement

Finally, eighty-three people were gathered in the Seafront's lounge: guests, chefs, chambermaids, bellboys and anyone else who happened to be in the hotel. When Alvin Bigshot informed them, amidst much throat-clearing, that a couple of floors above their heads a giant Fire Ghost was rampaging around, these eighty-three people took the news in a variety of ways.

Tom counted eighteen instances of fainting; forty-one hasty departures from the lounge followed by immediate suitcase-packing or cancelling of reservations without notice; three fits of mad rage; and six demands for compensation.

There remained only fifteen people: two chefs, two chambermaids, one bellboy and ten guests who, for a variety of reasons, weren't prepared to leave the hotel.

Firstly, there was the bellboy the ghosthunters had rescued from the linen cupboard. By way of thanks, he offered to help the trio, much to Tom's astonishment. Then there were the chefs, who felt that as they'd already survived an encounter with a little Fire Ghost, there was no need for them to run away from a bigger one. The chambermaids had no desire to lose their jobs over a rumour of a ghost. And as for the ten remaining guests, six of them thought that at last something interesting was going to happen to liven up their dull

holidays. The remaining four just didn't believe in ghosts: they suspected a complete and utter swindle on the part of the hotel management.

While the manager gloomily watched his guests fleeing, Tom and Hetty Hyssop were waiting impatiently for the fax from Mr Lovely.

Hugo found this all far too boring, so he went off to scare a few guests while they were packing their cases, before rummaging around in the cellar for a while.

When Mr Lovely's fax finally arrived, Tom and Hetty Hyssop sat themselves down on one of the wonderfully squidgy sofas in the hotel foyer, though Tom could have easily done without the brightly burning fireplace, which reminded him all too much of their last encounter with the ghost they would soon have to face again.

'Any sockets around here?' asked Hetty Hyssop.

'Two,' replied Tom. 'But both secured with icing!'

'Good, then start reading. I don't have my reading glasses with me!'

At the top of the first page, Mr Lovely had written:

Extract from *The Big Ghost Encyclopaedia*, Volume 23:

THE GILIG
(GRUESOME INVINCIBLE LIGHTNING GHOST)
Species: **Fire Ghost**

All ghost experts agree that exactly five types of ghost belong in Danger Category One. The GILIG is one of the five.

It is capable of a terrifying number of things; unfortunately, nothing more precise than this is known because most people attacked by GILIGs have not survived. However, it is known that GILIGs are capable of melting any inorganic matter such as stone, metal or glass, most probably showing a particular preference for metal. GILIGs can turn animals and humans to ashes, shrivel them up, or turn them into something similar to themselves, namely a Category One or Category Two Fire Ghost. They primarily seem to prefer the last option.

Buildings attacked by GILIGs are typically left in a state of total devastation after one or two weeks. Beware of violent storms: GILIGS clearly prefer to materialise through flashes of lightning and usually invade a building structure through its telephone wires. Beware, too, of sockets: during a GILIG attack, lethal flashes of lightning or highly toxic vapour can escape through them at any moment. Anyone exposed to the ghostly fire of a GILIG for longer than a quarter of an hour will find that his skin turns orange – which not only lasts a long time and looks disgusting but also, unfortunately, gives off a very unpleasant smell. Other effects of a GILIG encounter are extreme hair growth and the tip of the nose turning red.

Protective Measures During a GILIG Attack

It can only be urged that even the most experienced ghosthunters do not attempt to drive out a GILIG. All such undertakings thus far have ended with the unfortunate ghosthunter either being turned to ashes or transformed into a minor Fire Ghost. A most miserable existence, the reader can be assured. Should there be no possibility of immediate escape, we recommend that the ghosthunter organise a Fire Ghost-proof room in the cellar. Most ghosts, it is true, are notoriously keen on cellars, but all types of Fire Ghost are a remarkable exception to this. Since cellar rooms are usually decidedly cold, Fire Ghosts (including the GILIG) prefer to inhabit cellars with central-heating boilers, saunas, or a heated games room, which therefore should under no circumstances be used as a hiding place. If, though, a wine cellar is available in the building under attack, this is the ideal place of refuge. For GILIGs have just one known weakness: they are allergic to alcohol.

GILIGs can, it is true, be scared off by traditional anti-Fire Ghost measures (sugar, cold air, handheld vacuum cleaners), but only alcohol will work for more than a minute on these absolutely vile ghosts. Should a GILIG come into contact with alcohol, it demonstrates dizziness as well as the tendency to dissolve and shrivel up.

The use of alcohol has admittedly never been enough on its own to drive out a GILIG as far as is known. If, however, it is a case of saving life and limb, alcohol is currently the only known method. Unfortunately, no research has been done into which kind of alcohol has the most powerful effect. All experiments of this type were abruptly terminated by the GILIGs themselves.

Summary

Should you have the misfortune to witness or become the victim of a GILIG attack, flee at once! Do not – repeat, not – try to drive it out! Never in the whole history of ghosthunting has such an attempt been successful!

Tom raised his head. 'That was the first extract . . . shall I carry on reading?'

Hetty Hyssop nodded and looked into the fire-place. 'Bad, bad, bad,' she muttered.

Tom took the second page of Mr Lovely's fax. At the top, it said:

Extract from *Milestones in Ghost Investigation*:

The famous ghosthunter Henry MacGhoul was, as the interested reader is bound to know, one of the few utterly fearless ghosthunters, one who primarily dedicated himself to investigating and fighting the notorious GILIG. Unfortunately, Henry MacGhoul's investigations came to a most tragic end. One of the GILIGs he was observing turned him into a Category One Fire Ghost, and the most recent information on his whereabouts states that he is eking out a wretched existence in a gold mine. However, all modern-day ghosthunters owe a debt of gratitude to this courageous man for the small amount of interesting information now possessed about these dreadful GILIGs. For MacGhoul's notes, made just minutes before he was turned into a ghost, have all been preserved in full (give or take a couple of burned sections), and are currently held by RICOG (the Research Institute for COmbating Ghosts). These notes clearly indicate that GILIGs are frightened of one particular substance: the extremely disgusting slime of a cold and completely harmless ghost, the so-called ASG.

Henry MacGhoul observed on several occasions that a GILIG cannot cross the slimy trail of an ASG.

Tom raised his head and looked at Hetty Hyssop.

'That,' she said, 'is very interesting indeed!'

'And we stopped Hugo from sliming all over the place!' cried Tom.

'Hmm, most regrettable,' said Hetty Hyssop.

Tom continued reading:

Zachary Lovely   23 Nightshade Walk

Milestones in Ghost Investigation

The more a GILIG comes into contact with ASG slime, the more peculiar becomes its behaviour. It starts to panic; its movements become chaotic and uncontrolled – and in the most extreme cases, it starts to perform the notorious GILIG pirouette. The following happens during this extremely terrifying ghostly event: the GILIG starts to whirl round faster and faster, accompanied by highly unpleasant noises. Its fiery energy is thus increased to such a vast extent that it drills itself into the ground and disappears. (This doesn't happen on very fine sand.) Then, from its subterranean location, it spirals upwards into the air and is hurled high into the atmosphere. The GILIG pirouette may possibly have other effects, but Henry MacGhoul's notes are, unfortunately, rendered illegible by burn marks and soot from this point forward, so it cannot be said for certain. All that can be hoped is that more precise information will be gained over the course of the coming years in this highly interesting yet exceedingly dangerous field.

Tom looked up. He and Hetty Hyssop exchanged a grim smile.

'I see a lot of work ahead for our ASG friend,' she said. 'But that's how we will do it!'

Tom looked around. 'Hugo won't like this at all,' he said. 'By the way, where's he gone?'

Hetty Hyssop pointed upwards. Sharp screams and Hugo's muffled ASG howls were coming from somewhere on the first floor.

'Let's allow him a bit of fun,' said Hetty Hyssop. 'And as for us, we need a bite to eat before we get seriously stuck into our work. Don't you agree?'

'Fantastic!' Tom sighed. 'My stomach already sounds as if I'm trying out ventriloquism!'

'Good.' Hetty Hyssop stood up and straightened her fire helmet. 'But let's just drop in on Bigshot on the way. I've got a little job for him as well!'

Ghosts in the Afternoon

They found Alvin Bigshot at reception, where guest after guest was handing back keys. The poor manager was so pale that he could have been taken for a ghost himself.

'Mr Bigshot,' said Hetty Hyssop, standing next to him. 'Presumably you have a wine cellar?'

The manager pulled a worried face. 'Of course. Er, why? This ghost surely isn't . . .'

'No, no,' Hetty Hyssop reassured him. 'Quite the reverse. As we've found out in the meantime, that's the last place it'll end up. So we'll use the wine cellar as our meeting room and safe place. I'd like you to take all the remaining personnel and guests there, since it's just a matter of time before the **GILIG** changes floors, and we can't possibly keep an eye on all the rooms. What's more, please make sure everyone has your express permission to use champagne and wine bottles as instruments of defence if they are attacked by the GILIG!'

'It just gets better and better!' moaned Alvin Bigshot. 'You're seriously trying to tell me that we can chase this monstrosity away by smashing bottles on its head?'

'Oh, don't be silly!' said Hetty Hyssop. 'But according to our information, alcohol scares it off, so don't make such a fuss. We're relying on you. Got it?'

Alvin Bigshot merely looked down at the ground in despair.

'We're going to get something to eat,' said Tom. 'If Hugo comes down, could you send him to find us?'

'Oh yes, and one more thing!' Hetty Hyssop lowered her voice. 'There's no reason to look so despairing, Bigshot. We're confident that we'll be able to solve your enormous little problem before too long.'

'What? How? Really?' The manager immediately regained a touch of colour.

'Shhh!' Hetty Hyssop put a finger to her lips. 'Tell you everything later!'

Then she and Tom disappeared into the dining room.

They ordered the largest set menu on offer (on the house, naturally), but even after they had eaten their way through all the courses, there was still no sign of Hugo.

'That pleasure-mad ASG!' Hetty Hyssop looked around. 'We shouldn't have given him those tinted glasses. Without them he'd at least behave better during the day!'

Only two other tables were occupied. At one of them sat a chubby red-haired lady named Alma Muddlebird, who considered Fire Ghosts to be an inspired holiday surprise. At the other table, Mr and Mrs Wadley were quarrelling; they had stayed because they thought the whole thing was a complete and utter swindle. The pair of them were so brown from sunbathing that they looked like dried prunes. Every now and then they cast evil looks at the ghosthunters – not that it bothered Hetty and Tom.

'A stroke of luck that the two chefs stayed behind,' said Tom, his mouth full.

'You need a bit of luck every now and then!' Hetty Hyssop helped herself to her third portion of raspberry pudding and poured a bit more of the quite delicious chocolate sauce over it.

Then she suddenly sat bolt upright.

'Can you smell something?' she asked.

Tom sniffed. 'Smells like someone's been playing with fire!' he said worriedly.

'Precisely. What a pain! You can't even eat your dinner in peace!' Hetty Hyssop sprang up. 'Quick!' she cried to the other guests. 'Grab some bottles of champagne from the buffet – and all the sugar you can find! We're about to have visitors!'

Alma Muddlebird clapped excitedly and ran over to the buffet. The Wadleys, however, didn't stir from their table.

'Ridiculous!' declared Mr Wadley, slurping his mineral water. 'How stupid do you think we are?'

The burning smell grew stronger.

Tom grabbed the icing baster, and Hetty Hyssop put three bottles of champagne and a full sugar bowl on the table.

'If alcohol works on the GILIG,' she whispered to Tom, 'then it might work on the smaller ghosts too, and I reckon that's what we're about to be dealing with!'

At that very moment, three empty tables rose up

into the air. The table tops turned to ashes, and five little Fire Ghosts shot out from between the burning table legs. Screeching and hissing like fireworks, they raced towards the guests.

Mr Wadley's mineral water evaporated on his lips, and Mrs Wadley's fork melted in her hand. With flickering fingers, the Fire Ghosts grabbed both of them by the hair – knocking off Mr Wadley's wig, which exploded on the floor – and blackened them from top to bottom with soot.

'Shake the champagne and uncork it!' Hetty Hyssop cried to Alma Muddlebird, who was standing on the table with her mouth open and the bottle in her hand.

Bang! The corks hit the ceiling, and champagne showered the Fire Ghosts' hot bodies. Reeling, they fluttered down to the floor, as yellow as lemons and clearly much cooler.

'Fetch us a Thermos flask!' cried Hetty Hyssop to the bellboy who was leaning against the wall as if turned to stone. 'Quickly!'

Tom grabbed the sugar and shook it all over the stunned Fire Ghosts.

Alma Muddlebird cast aside her empty champagne bottle, jumped up from her table ready for action, and buried the Fire Ghost who was whizzing around her table under a mountain of sugar.

'Brilliant!' cried Hetty Hyssop. 'You're a natural!'

Alma Muddlebird turned as red as her hair. The Wadleys, however, were cowering under their table, trembling.

'Champagne's a one hundred per cent success!' Tom grinned. He slipped on his oven gloves and caught the two Fire Ghosts who were just about to reel through the wall. They were as warm as freshly baked bread rolls.

'How many have you got?' asked Hetty.

'Two!'

'I've got two as well!' With the aid of a napkin, Alma Muddlebird pulled a squealing Fire Ghost out from under the ice cream menu.

'Yours plus mine makes five!' asserted Hetty Hyssop. 'And we've already got Mrs Redmond. So there's only one missing now!' She looked around searchingly. 'Where have those Thermos flasks got to?'

The bellboy who was supposed to fetch them was still rooted to the spot, his lips trembling as if they were

73

still searching for the right words to describe what he had just seen.

'Tom, nip into the manager's office!' cried Hetty Hyssop. 'There are a couple there that I prepared earlier. But be quick. I don't know when these little beasts will start to heat up again!'

With record-breaking speed, Tom whizzed through the hotel foyer, a wobbly lemon-coloured ghost in each hand.

'Can't stop!' he panted as he swept past the baffled Alvin Bigshot. Once in the office, he stuffed his prisoners into two of the Thermos flasks, which were all neatly lined up; then he crammed three more flasks under his arm and raced back.

He was just in time. Alma Muddlebird's prisoners had already turned dark orange.

As soon as the ghosts were safely in the flasks, the red-haired lady poured herself a glass of water and stuck her hot fingers in it.

'Wow, that was exciting!' she sighed.

'We're most grateful for your help!' Hetty Hyssop replied, smiling at her.

'Oh, really?' Alma Muddlebird murmured, and returned the smile shyly.

The Wadleys, meanwhile, were still hiding under their table. Tom and Hetty Hyssop left them there and went to take the Thermos flasks back to Mr Bigshot's office.

Just as they were crossing the hotel foyer, Hugo came wobbling down the stairs, his fireman's helmet in his hand and a top hat on his head.

'You've timed it well again,' said Tom by way of greeting. 'Where were you all that time? And where did you get that hat?'

'Pah – nothing to do with yoooooou!' breathed Hugo, and floated into Alvin Bigshot's office with them. 'But if yooooou're really desperate to know – it looks pretty bad on the third floor now tooooo. Give it a miss, it's all hot and stinky, cor bloimey. Oi turned my back on it roight away, just took the hat. Funny, that. Rolled down the stairs, roight after me!'

'And what about the second floor?' Hetty Hyssop put the Thermos flasks containing their prisoners on Alvin Bigshot's desk. 'Is the GILIG already there too, Hugo?'

'Nooooo!' said Hugo, wobbling to the aquarium to scare the fish.

'Good!' Sighing, Hetty Hyssop sank down on to

Alvin Bigshot's managerial office chair. 'Then hopefully we'll have a bit of time. Especially you, Hugo!'

'Meeee? Why meeee?' Hugo turned faintly pink.

'Because we need tons of ASG slime,' said Tom with a slightly mean grin. 'Whole bucketloads. So take off your shoes and get sliming!'

A Shock in the Evening

Hugo spent the whole afternoon wobbling around on the edge of a big bathtub. By the time darkness fell, the bath was full to the brim with glistening, sticky ASG slime, and Hugo's feet were hurting. Grumpily, he retreated to a built-in cupboard whilst Tom and Hetty Hyssop transferred the slime into buckets. They hauled one bucketful down to the cellar in order to paint the door with it. In the meantime all sixteen people, including Alvin Bigshot, had made their way down there, for Alma Muddlebird and the Wadleys had described the events in the dining room so graphically that even the most hard-boiled unbelievers no longer felt secure in their rooms. But, as Hetty Hyssop always said, you never know with ghosts. Therefore all the cellar-dwellers were given bottles of champagne to hold – the cheapest kind, naturally – and a sugar bowl. They could be in for a very, very unpleasant night. Nobody doubted it for a minute . . .

Four more buckets of ASG slime were stowed away behind reception so that they could be used later for more painting. And, finally, Tom and Hetty Hyssop lugged a couple of buckets down to the beach. Hugo followed them, yawning. The sun hung red and fiery over the sea, and the waves made a faint squelching sound as they lapped the damp sand.

'Has all the water in the hotel been turned off?' asked Hetty Hyssop. 'Not that the GILIG is going to get its strength back by having a shower!'

'No worries. It's all off,' said Tom.

The sun sank into the sea, sending a kind of liquid fire across the waves.

'The tide's coming in at the moment. The water's still rising, so there's no point smearing slime along the edge!' Hetty Hyssop drew a line in the sand with her foot. 'I'd guess the tide will come in this far, so we'll paint the slime up to here, Hugo. The GILIG can come up to this line, and not one slobbery step further. Empty all the buckets, and if it comes, put some fresh slime on top of the old slime too. If the GILIG gets into the sea, we're all goners. Got it?'

'Yeah, yeah, oi'm not stupid,' snorted Hugo, offended. 'Yooooou lure it here first. Oi'll take care of the rest!'

'Or so we hope,' muttered Tom, looking up at the hotel. The windows of the fourth and third floors were illuminated red, and for a moment he thought he could see a suspicious flickering on the second floor too. But when he looked more closely it had disappeared.

'Go on then, you lay your trail, Hugo,' said Hetty Hyssop. 'And remember not to spill any on the steps over there. It has to come this way and only this way, OK?'

'Oi might run out of sloime!' Hugo gave a hollow laugh.

'Never mind your stupid jokes,' said Hetty Hyssop. 'This ghost puts me right off laughing. Come on, Tom – we'll go and take care of the foyer and the lounge!'

But Tom stood as if rooted to the spot. He was staring up at the second floor again. 'Look up there!' he whispered. 'Fourth room on the left. There's someone running around with a candle!'

Hetty Hyssop and Hugo turned and looked up. Tom was right. Behind the fourth balcony door there was a light flickering, and a dark shadow was moving through the room.

'That's Mr Zimmerman's room!' cried Hetty Hyssop. 'He was moaning in the cellar about having forgotten his false teeth. Surely he wouldn't be mad enough to go back up for them?'

At that point, a light went on in Mr Zimmerman's room.

'Oh yes, he *is* mad enough,' said Tom. 'What do you reckon? Should Hugo and I get him out of there?'

'Oh no. Yooooou're on yooooour own now!' Hugo shrivelled up. 'Oi'm totally whacked from all that sloiming!'

'Oh, come on, don't make a fuss,' said Tom. 'We'll just fly up there quickly, cop hold of this Zimmerman, and send him back to the cellar. Who knows how he might otherwise get in our way later on!'

'Oh, OK!' moaned Hugo, clasping Tom under his arm and floating up to Mr Zimmerman's balcony.

They weren't quite there when the balcony door suddenly flew open and Mr Zimmerman leaned over the rails, shrieking. He was holding a bottle of champagne in his left hand and his false teeth in his right.

'Help!' he bellowed. 'Help! The gh – gho – ghost!'

At the same moment a fiery glow poured through the balcony door.

'Quick, Hugo!' Tom yelled.

The GILIG stuck its huge head out of the open door, grinned, and stretched its burning fingers out towards Mr Zimmerman.

'Get lost!' cried the old man, tugging at the champagne cork. *Pop!* The cork plopped into the sand below, and frothy champagne squirted on to the fiery hand.

'Aaaaaaaarrrrrrggggggggggggghhhhhhhhhh!' howled the GILIG, licking the champagne from its fingers with its gigantic tongue. Then it emitted a threatening growl.

The GILIG didn't seem to notice Tom and Hugo

at all. It kept on licking its hand, hissing and snarling. As for Mr Zimmerman, his eyes nearly popped out of his head with horror when he saw the inflated Hugo floating over the railings. He almost fell off the balcony with shock.

With one leap, Tom was at his side.

'Don't worry!' he said. 'It's just an ASG!'

ASG! Tom had barely spoken the word when the GILIG raised its head with a start. And once again, Tom looked into its hideous eyes. This time they were black, as black as coal and as dark as hell. Tom's legs started to tremble ever so slightly.

'Hugo!' he cried. He pressed his icing baster with trembling fingers – but nothing came out. Not even the tiniest squirt. 'Hugo!' Tom's voice cracked. 'Get us down, quickly!'

'He's gone!' whispered Mr Zimmerman hoarsely. 'Your ghost friend has gone!'

Tom looked round disbelievingly. But it was true. No sign of Hugo. Tom's heart began to pound.

The GILIG carried on staring at him. Now it wasn't just licking its fingers, but its lips too. It breathed on Tom, and Tom's face began to tingle under the special paste, as if someone were sticking thousands of red-hot needles into it.

'Whaaaaat's aaaaall thiiiiiis aaaaabout aaaaan AAAAASG?' whispered the GILIG. Tom had never in his life heard anything more grisly than this whispering. 'Wheeeeere iiiiis thiiiiiis foooooliiiiish AAAAASG? I'll vaaaaapooooooriiiiiseeeee iiiiit!'

'Oh no yoooooou won't!' Hugo's hand emerged from under the balcony like white smoke, and ran its slimy fingers across the railing. Quick as a flash, his hugely long and wobbly arms snaked round Tom and Mr Zimmerman. Then Hugo simply picked them up and carried them away.

Berserk with rage, the GILIG blazed after them, but when it stretched its fiery arms across the railings it fell back, howling, and started scratching as if it had fleas.

'Hahahahahahaha!' cried Hugo triumphantly. 'Hahahahahahahaha! Just loooook at yourself. Ha!'

The sun sank into the sea, turning the sky red. The GILIG on the balcony, however, just went pale and then vanished, as if someone had switched off a light.

Hugo gently deposited Tom and Mr Zimmerman on the sand by Hetty Hyssop.

'Mr Zimmerman, how *could* you cause us so much trouble?' The ghosthunter laid right into him. 'My assistants risked life and limb for you. Life and limb!'

'But my false teeth!' cried Mr Zimmerman, holding his dentures right under her nose. 'I *had* to have them!'

'Well, you certainly won't need them once you're a Fire Ghost!' Hetty Hyssop looked anxiously up at Mr Zimmerman's balcony. There was no sign of the GILIG.

'I don't like this,' hissed Hetty Hyssop. 'It'll be very angry. Hopefully it's not already on its way down. That'd scupper our entire plan!' She grabbed Tom's arm. 'Come on, we must spread the slime around the hotel. Hugo, you get everything ready here on the beach.'

'OK,' said Hugo, and wobbled casually across the sand. Wherever his white feet walked, they left a glistening trail of slime.

Tom and Hetty Hyssop hurried back to the hotel together with the remorseful Mr Zimmerman. As they crossed the dining room, he inserted his false teeth shamefacedly.

'Zimmerman, go down to the cellar and be quick

about it,' said Hetty Hyssop as they entered the dark hotel foyer. 'And tell the others down there that if I catch sight of any of them up here, I'll *personally* turn them into Fire Ghosts.'

Mr Zimmerman shot off, and Tom and Hetty Hyssop were left alone in the hall. The burning smell had meanwhile become so strong that it made it hard to breathe.

'Come on, Tom,' said Hetty Hyssop. 'We've not got a moment to lose. I reckon this GILIG will be so angry after its mishap on the balcony that it'll come down without us having to lure it.' They retrieved the four buckets of ASG slime from behind reception and, using a large paintbrush, spread the contents over all the doors. The only door left un-beslimed was the one to the lounge, which led out to the veranda and the beach. Then they painted all the skirting boards, smeared the carpets and walls, and finally plunged their hands into the bucket, now practically empty.

'Yuk!' groaned Tom. 'Is that disgusting or what? I hope I'll be able to get this stuff off later on.'

Side by side, they stood in the doorway to the lounge. The hotel was filled with a deathly silence.

'That GILIG seems to have been scared good and

proper,' whispered Hetty Hyssop. 'I'd never have thought we'd have to wait so long for it!'

'It can take its time so far as I'm concerned,' Tom whispered back. But then he suddenly felt the room turning warm, very warm. As warm as an oven.

'It's coming!' cried Hetty Hyssop.

And the GILIG came.

Fireworks!

irst of all the ceiling changed colour. Soot tumbled down, and brown burn marks started to spread like ink on blotting paper. Then flames leaped down the walls and crept from all directions towards Tom and Hetty Hyssop like hideous animals. The lift door sprang open and clouds of yellow smoke billowed out, acrid and stinking. Hastily the ghosthunters put on their nose clips – which was not easy with slimy fingers – and stared at the lift.

But the GILIG didn't come out of the lift.

No: it burst from the ceiling. Glowing red and fiery, it fell down – and for the first time, the ghosthunters got a clear view of it. Its legs were short and bandy and had difficulty carrying its plump body. Its arms hung down to its knees, and its vast head was stuck, neckless, between its hunched and crooked shoulders.

'Zzzzzzzzzzzzzzrrrrrrrrrrhhhhhhhh!' growled the GILIG, baring its teeth. It shook its fiery mane and looked around. Its gaze lingered on Tom and Hetty Hyssop.

Tom's legs wanted to run away, outside, just any-where so long as it was away from the murderous heat and that terrible Lightning Ghost, which appeared to grow with every breath it took. But Tom stayed where he was. Just as he had promised. For they were the bait that would lure the GILIG out on to the soft sand, where Hugo's slime would force it to do the GILIG pirouette.

Their plan seemed to work. The GILIG came stamping over to them. With its third step, one of its fiery toes trod in Hugo's slime. Howling, it lifted up its foot, scratched itself like mad and, enraged, shot a jet of flame at Tom and Hetty Hyssop. They both ducked just in time.

'Slimy regards,' cried Tom. 'Slimy regards from our ASG!'

'Sssshhhsssshhhssshhhrrrrraaaaaa!' snarled the GILIG, and made a huge leap for the ghosthunters.

'Come on!' cried Hetty Hyssop.

Tom didn't need a second invitation. Side by side they raced through the lounge, knocking over chairs and bumping into tables and flowerpots, until they were out on the veranda. Below them on the sand, shimmering a bluish white in the moonlight, Hugo was waiting for them.

Out of breath and coughing from the smoke, Tom and Hetty Hyssop stumbled down the steps to the beach. They could already feel the GILIG's hot breath on their necks, but they didn't turn round until they were standing next to Hugo. Like a giant ball of fire, the GILIG sprang on its bandy legs from the veranda down on to the sand, right in the middle of the circle that Hugo had drawn with his shimmering slime. Snarling, it looked round, jumped from left to right and back again, and could find no way out.

'Ha! So how d'yooooou loike that, then?' mocked Hugo, stretching contentedly in the moonlight.

The GILIG jumped around in the sand, bellowing. It jumped faster and faster until it was spinning like a top, howling hideously as it span. And with every spin it became thinner and longer, until it was nothing but a twirling column of fire reaching ever higher into the sky.

'Nearly,' whispered Hetty Hyssop. 'We've nearly done it!'

But then, all of a sudden, the GILIG braced its

glowing arms in the air, slowed its twirling and howling, shrivelled up again, and stopped with a jolt. It paused, unmoving, its back to the ghosthunters. Then it turned dark red, so dark red that only its silhouette was visible in the night.

Hetty Hyssop pulled Tom a few steps backwards,

and even Hugo wasn't floating quite so near to the Lightning Ghost now.

They heard a faint growling, dark and threatening. Then the GILIG span round, its mouth wide open, and blew with all its remaining strength at Hugo's slimy trail. Its breath was as hot as liquid fire.

Tom put his hands protectively in front of his face. His skin was burning, his eyes were running, and his hair was so hot that he thought it would catch fire at any moment. Hugo wobbled back, howling.

'Watch out,' cried Hetty Hyssop. 'It's coming through!' The GILIG kept blowing, shrivelling more and more as it did so. But Hugo's slime was changing, too. It started hissing and steaming and then, quite suddenly, turned to ash.

Horrified, Tom and Hetty Hyssop drew back until they were standing in the water.

'We've had it!' whispered Hetty Hyssop.

By now, the GILIG was barely bigger than Tom – but it was free. And just a couple of metres away, the sea was lapping against the sand, glowing from the Lightning Ghost's hot breath.

'Juuuuust yooooouuuuu waaaaait!' it snarled.

Smoking and stinking, it sprang to the water, its fiery body diving into the waves. Then, like a jet of flame, it shot up into the black sky, higher and higher, until it was so massive that it blocked out the moon.

'Grrrrraaaaaaaaaa!' it growled menacingly, and stretched out its flaming arms.

The whole world seemed red and black, nothing more. But suddenly something green and shimmering appeared behind the GILIG's left knee.

'Hugo!' cried Tom. 'Get away from there! Go on! *Quickly!*'

But Hugo had no intention of going. He waved at Tom and Hetty and floated slowly up to the GILIG. Hetty Hyssop shook her head in disbelief.

'It'll vaporise him!' cried Tom in despair. 'We have to do something!'

But Hetty Hyssop just murmured, 'That ASG has got something up his sleeve. But what?'

The GILIG had meanwhile spotted Hugo as well. Taken aback, it peered down at him. Compared to the gigantic Lightning Ghost that stood there in the waves, blazing and still growing, Hugo looked like a white handkerchief being tossed around in the wind.

'Aaaaah, AAAAASG!' roared the GILIG. 'IIIII'll vaaaaapooooooriiiiiseeeee yooooouuuuu! Thaaaaat's whaaaaat IIIII'll dooooo!'

It batted at Hugo with its fiery hands as if he were a pesky fly. But the ASG kept deftly evading it.

Tom shuddered. The whole sea glowed blood red in the GILIG's ghostly light, and Hugo looked so terribly vulnerable, wobbling around those immense bandy legs. But he was evidently in the best of spirits.

'Vapoooorise? Vapoooorise? Don't make me laugh!' he cried hollowly, flying higher and higher, past the fiery fingers that were grabbing angrily at him, until he was floating right above the GILIG's flaming mane.

'Enjoy, yooooou vile baggage!' breathed Hugo. Then he spat on the gigantic ghost's head. Right on the very middle of its head.

'Aaaaaaaaaargh!' screeched the GILIG shrilly, inflating like a fiery hot-air balloon – and then bursting with a *bang* that shattered every window in the Seafront Hotel. Millions of fiery sparks rained down on the sea. Hugo was blown back to the beach, where he plopped down on the sand next to Tom.

'Unbelievable!' breathed Tom.

Red sparks were still raining down from the sky

and the whole night sparkled as if someone had lit a giant firework. Hugo was looking a bit singed in places, but otherwise seemed to be in the very best of ghostly health.

'So, how did I do?' he asked, inflating himself proudly.

'I don't get it!' cried Hetty Hyssop. 'I just don't get it. How did you know that your saliva would have such a catastrophic effect on that monster?'

'Oh, *that*!' Hugo nonchalantly wobbled around in front of her nose. 'It was obvious!'

'Nothing was obvious!' cried Tom. 'How did you know what to do?'

Hugo grinned. 'When yoooou told me all that stuff about the sloime, it became clear. My spit is miles more sloimy than my sloime. Much stickier and all. *Now* do you get it?'

'You pesky ASG!' Hetty Hyssop gave Hugo a friendly dig in the wobbly ribs. 'Why didn't you tell us?'

'Because oi loike suuuuurprises!' cried Hugo, turning a somersault in the air. 'And it was a pretty good suuuurprise, wasn't it?'

'Too right!' sighed Tom. 'It almost killed me, your

surprise. So just bear in mind next time that I don't like surprises half as much as you do, OK?'

'Spoilsport!' said Hugo, tapping Tom on the nose with an icy finger.

Then the three ghosthunters made their way back to the hotel, tired and slightly singed, but very happy.

The Idea that Saved the Day

Tom was given the job of telling all the inhabitants of the wine cellar that the GILIG had had it. Their cries of joy were quite deafening. One of the chefs carried the youngest ghosthunter back to the foyer on his shoulders, and Alvin Bigshot declared that Hyssop and Co. would be lifetime guests of honour at his hotel.

Then the rescued people all streamed out on to the beach, where little red sparks were still glimmering in the night air, to celebrate the success of the three ghosthunters by eating, drinking, dancing and singing. Hugo was disgusted. He thought that large groups of singing humans sounded far more hideous than any ghostly howling. Tom thought so too, and so the pair of them sat down on the sand slightly away from the noise and looked out to the sea, no longer red, where the moonlight was reflected in the waves like a silver path.

Hetty Hyssop and Alvin Bigshot didn't join in the celebrations either. They took a tour of inspection through the entire hotel, which confirmed that the Seafront really was ghost-free – apart from one tiny Fire Ghost which they discovered in a tooth mug and caught without any problems.

Other than that, the hotel was in a pretty sorry state. The walls, ceilings and furniture were all singed, sooty and covered in ash. Many of the door locks and room numbers had melted, and no cleaning fluid on earth could have removed the GILIG's footprints from the carpet.

As they made their way back down in the badly damaged lift, Alvin Bigshot burst into tears. The tears ran down his cheeks and dropped off his moustache.

'I'm ruined!' he sobbed. 'Completely ruined!'

'Come, come, my dear chap,' said Hetty Hyssop, patting him sympathetically on the shoulder. 'That's no reason to go to pieces. You're insured, aren't you?'

'Against ghosts?' snivelled the manager. 'Of course not!'

Hetty Hyssop shook her head. 'That's very remiss of you. All large buildings should be insured against ghosts. Large buildings are particularly attractive to all types of ghostly things!'

'But I didn't know!' moaned the manager. 'How's a normal person supposed to know that, I ask you?'

The lift door opened with a faint squeak, and the pair went out into the hotel foyer. The celebrations were still going on outside.

'Shall we go out?' asked Hetty Hyssop.

But Alvin Bigshot just shook his head sadly. 'I don't feel like celebrating!'

'Fine, then let's go to your office. I've got to lock up this thing anyway!' Hetty Hyssop said, holding up the last captive Fire Ghost. She took the manager, who was quietly sobbing to himself, by the arm. 'If you make us a cup of coffee,' she said, pulling him gently along with her, 'I'll tell you what we can do to save your hotel from ruin!'

'Really?' Alvin Bigshot looked at her, astonished. 'You mean you've got an idea?'

'Oh yes, and I think it's a good one, too,' said Hetty Hyssop.

With a sigh Alvin Bigshot opened the office door.

'Hello, Beegshottykeens!' Hugo was sitting in the

manager's chair, resting his mouldy green feet on the
desk.

'Come on, Hugo, get down,' said Tom. He was
slumped in another chair, looking rather tired.

'What are you two doing here?' asked Hetty
Hyssop. 'Didn't you want to celebrate?'

Tom shook his head and yawned.

'Me noither!' said Hugo, and wobbled out of Alvin Bigshot's seat. 'People kept wanting to shake my hand and say thank yoooou. It made my fingers horribly warm. Disgusting!'

Alvin Bigshot went to his coffee machine. 'Dear Hetty Hyssop, would you mind telling me your idea?'

'Of course.' Hetty Hyssop stuffed the Fire Ghost into the last empty Thermos flask and sat on the edge of the desk. 'Well, this is what I thought: you should just turn the Seafront Hotel into a ghost hotel!'

The manager dropped his coffee filter in surprise. 'A what?' he asked, shaking the coffee grounds out of his shoe.

'A ghost hotel,' repeated Hetty Hyssop. 'Here's what I had in mind: you save a fortune on the renovation costs by leaving the melted locks and door numbers as they are. I'd also leave the footprints on the carpet; that sort of thing's very effective. Oh, and I wouldn't even bother clearing the soot and ashes away in some of the rooms, because these could be the five-star Fire Ghost Suites: genuine ghostliness guaranteed!'

'I get it!' Alvin Bigshot tugged excitedly at his moustache. 'Yes, I get it – please carry on!'

Hetty Hyssop smiled. 'With great pleasure. Next you engage the services of a few harmless ghosts as waiters in the dining room. I'd recommend COHAGs (COmpletely HArmless Ghosts). A good friend of mine runs a ghost employment agency, and I'm sure he'd be glad to help you out. And finally you could ask our dear Hugo here if he wouldn't mind dropping in for a weekend every now and then to produce some nocturnal spookery. He's the perfect ghost for that kind of job!'

Flattered, Hugo turned purple. 'Oi'd be deloighted, in return for a comfy little spot in the cellar!'

'That's not a bad idea,' said Tom.

'Not a bad idea?' cried Alvin Bigshot. 'Not a bad idea? It's a brilliant idea! However can I thank you, my dear Mrs Hyssop?' He flung his arms around her neck.

'No thanks necessary, Alvin,' said Hetty Hyssop, gently disentangling herself from his embrace. 'I'm just glad that things have turned out so well. Though we've almost forgotten something!'

The others looked at her in surprise.

'Your guests!' Hetty Hyssop gesticulated at the seven Thermos flasks. 'We've still got to turn them back into humans!'

'But can it be done?' asked the manager, astonished.

'Oh, yes. It's not all that easy, and it takes a fair while, but it works fine. We need cotton wool, peppermint-flavoured icing, and a good dose of patience. I'd say,' she looked around, 'that as there's no way we'll sleep anyway, we might as well get it done now. What do you think, gentlemen?'

Ghosts from the Coffeepot

ugo wasn't keen to help with the de-ghosting. He felt that he'd already worked hard enough to last him at least a hundred years, and wobbled off to find himself a comfy little spot in the cellar where he could dream of his heroic deeds.

The other three got straight down to work. Alvin Bigshot gathered all the ingredients they needed, while Tom and Hetty Hyssop covered his desk in newspaper. Icing is, after all, pretty sticky stuff.

'Ready?' asked Hetty Hyssop, putting on her oven gloves.

'Ready,' said Tom and Alvin Bigshot. They likewise put on their gloves, and then they each took a Thermos flask.

The ghosts, cooled in dry ice, seemed extremely sleepy. They just fidgeted a bit when they were pulled out of their prisons.

Tom held his ghost right up to his eyes. 'I think I

spy Mrs Redmond,' he remarked. 'Ow! She bit my finger!'

'Yes, yes!' said Alvin Bigshot with a little smile. 'Mrs Redmond was always rather . . . how should I put it? Inclined to be snappy!'

Cautiously he inspected the ghost wriggling in his hand. 'Oh, I've clearly got Doctor Stickybeak, the ear, nose and throat specialist!'

'And who've I got?' Hetty Hyssop stuck her Fire Ghost under his nose.

'That's Miss Amanda Petalpottle, a quite charming elderly lady, though she doesn't look it at the moment!'

'Right, then,' said Hetty Hyssop, dipping a wad of cotton wool into a large bowl that was filled to the brim with icing. 'First we have to daub icing on the back of the head and shoulders. It's better not to do the face, because peppermint oil stings the eyes. Then we need to coat the trunk and arms, then the legs last of all. Needless to say, you don't have to cover every square inch with icing, but the layer needs to be quite thick.'

'And what happens when the ghost is all coated?' asked the manager, coating Doctor Stickybeak from head to toe in icing.

'Then,' said Hetty Hyssop, 'we put him on the desk. The sugar stops him floating off, and in four to five hours – so by dawn – he'll have turned into a human again.'

'Most interesting,' murmured Alvin Bigshot, putting the doctor, who was looking pretty furious, next to the aquarium. 'I must say, I'm glad I wasn't turned into a Fire Ghost!'

Tom had finished with Mrs Redmond too, and put her next to the iced doctor.

Thus they dealt with Mr Oswald Autocue, a famous television presenter, Mrs Hammerstein and her son Wolfgang, who almost burned off the tip of Hetty Hyssop's nose, and Mr Fotheringay-Popplescrunch, who was by all accounts such an unpleasant guest that Alvin Bigshot would have preferred to have left him in the Thermos flask.

When, finally, all the captive Fire Ghosts were iced and sitting on the desk, Tom and Hetty Hyssop felt so tired that they decided to put their heads down after all. The manager was extremely sorry that he couldn't offer them each an undamaged bed, but he made up two very comfortable loungers, complete with woollen blankets and pillows, which the two ghosthunters took with them into the room next to his office.

Alvin Bigshot, meanwhile, went out to see his guests and staff, who were still celebrating on the beach.

'Hetty . . .' said Tom, as they lay wrapped up next to each other on the loungers. 'We only just made it this time, didn't we?'

'A very narrow squeak indeed,' said Hetty Hyssop, and yawned. 'You don't mess around with GILIGs. As soon as we get home, I'm going to write to the *Big Ghost Encyclopaedia* and pass on our information. It needs to be accessible to all ghosthunters as quickly as possible!'

Tom giggled. 'True, but they aren't all lucky enough to work with an ASG. How are they supposed to get hold of the slime and the saliva?'

'That, thankfully, is not my problem!' sighed Hetty Hyssop, shutting her eyes.

'Are there really four other types of ghost that are as terrible as this GILIG?' asked Tom.

'There certainly are,' answered Hetty sleepily. 'I'd categorise two of them as being even more dangerous. But I shan't tell you about them now, or you'll be too frightened to sleep!'

'Really?' murmured Tom, pulling the covers right

up to his nose. 'Even more dangerous? Can't imagine that!'

And then, suddenly, he fell asleep.

In Case of
an Encounter

A vid readers, you now know in indisputable and occasionally crispy detail the dangers Tom withstood throughout his limb- and life-threatening ordeal with the GILIG of *Ghosthunters and the Gruesome Invincible Lightning Ghost!* Ergo (and hence) surely you would never be so adventurous and unabashedly rash as to ever attempt to extinguish such a conflagrant phantom yourselves.

However . . .

In the extremely improbable case of an unexpected and unprovoked encounter with a GILIG – or with one of its lesser relatives, a Fire Ghost – or even with a seemingly harmless, run-of-the-mill, not-really-so-scary spectre – the neophyte ghosthunter would be wise to take the following counsel into consideration:

PRECAUTIONARY MEASURES
Against Ghosts in General

• The colour red – as in socks, pullovers, curtains, sofas, etc.

• Raw eggs, for throwing.

• Violet-scented perfume: many species of ghost detest the smell. It makes their skin itch, and it has the added bonus of combating their natural and naturally foul ghost odour. For best results, spritz via an atomiser.

• Mirrors: hang them on your red-painted walls; wear pocket-sized varieties when in the field.

• A spare pair of shoes: depending on the variety of ghost, it will leave a trail that's sticky, snowy, muddy, etc. If in the thrill of the chase your shoes get glued in place, it helps to have a back-up pair.

• Graveyard earth that's been gathered at night (*see* Ghosthunters and the Incredibly Revolting Ghost! *for specifics*).

• And no matter what, do not – do NOT – carry a torch on ghosthunting expeditions. The beam of a torch will drive a ghost into a violent rage.

IN CASE OF AN ENCOUNTER WITH AN FG
(Fire Ghost)

• Outfit yourself with aviator goggles and a firefighter's helmet.

• Construct a suit from aluminium foil and coat with a paste made of equal parts SPF 30 sunscreen and sugared olive oil: the inconvenient stickiness will be less bothersome if you sporadically pause to recall the oven-roasted alternative.

• Line your shoes with squares of aluminium foil folded thirteen times over: any less will result in . . . well, let's just say it's no walk on the beach.

• Wear a nose clip: otherwise the smoky, sweet-and-sour stench of a Fire Ghost will cause the eyes to fill with tears, and subsequently, the aviator goggles to fill with water (*note: a small number of non-nose-clip-wearing ghosthunters also report the additional side effect of an inexplicable craving for a Chinese takeaway*).

• Pack a hairdryer and a baking tray: the former can be used to blow an FG to a safe and manageable distance; the latter, due to its heat-resistant properties, is good for bonking ghosts on their red-hot heads.

- Blast it with a baster-load of cake icing: a squirtful of sugar helps the Fire Ghost go down.
- Soak it with a splash of champagne – preferably French, though domestic vintages and even common Chardonnays will do in an emergency.
- Pick up the dazed FG with oven gloves; even when doused, it will still be too hot to handle bare-handed.
- Trap the wilted spirit in a Thermos flask until ready to convert it back to human form (*instructions follow*).
- And remember, do not – do NOT – attack an FG with liquid oxide of hydrogen (*or, as it is more commonly known, water*). Contrary to all that is logical, H_2O actually makes Fire Ghosts grow.

TO DE-GHOST AN FG TO ITS ORIGINAL HUMAN FORM

- Cover your work area with newspaper.
- Wearing oven gloves, dip a wad of cotton wool into a bowl of peppermint icing.
- Beginning with the back of the head and daubing downwards, coat the captured Fire Ghost with the

peppermint icing. The layer need not cover every square inch of the FG, but it ought to be thick.

• Allow to sit on the newspaper for up to five hours, or until the de-ghosting is complete.

IN CASE OF AN ENCOUNTER WITH A GILIG
(Gruesome Invincible LIghtning Ghost)

• Plug up all electrical sockets with icing: this will significantly hinder a GILIG's ability both to eavesdrop and to emit toxic vapours and sparks.

• Organise a safe room in a cellar: GILIGs are repelled by the cold, not to mention the potential proximity of champagne.

• Fill all available buckets and bathtubs with ASG slime (*note: to procure, it is first necessary to have an ASG on hand; contact Hyssop & Co. to enquire about our reasonable ASG rental rates*).

• Cover all surfaces with the ASG slime: upon treading in the goo, a GILIG will ideally convulse into its idiosyncratic pirouette, drilling itself into oblivion. Either that, or it will incinerate the slime on the spot, then be all the more enraged by your amateur attempts to quench it.

• When all else fails, hit it with spit: the only known substance with one hundred per cent proven effectiveness in extinguishing GILIGs is not the slime but rather the saliva of an ASG (*note: Hyssop & Co.'s 2-for-1 slime/saliva discount package is available all year round, though higher prices apply during peak hurricane season*).

Indispensable Alphabetical
APPENDIX OF ASSORTED GHOSTS

ASG	**A**veragely **S**pooky **G**host
BB	**B**loody **B**aroness
BLAGDO	**BLA**ck Ghost **DO**gs
BOSG	**BO**g and **S**wamp **G**host
CG	**C**ellar **G**host
COHAG	**CO**mpletely **HA**rmless **G**host
FG	**F**ire **G**host
FOFIFO	**FO**ggy **FI**gure **FO**rmer
FOFUG	**FO**ggy **FU**g-**G**host
GG	**G**raveyard **G**host
GHADAP	**GH**ost with **A DA**rk **P**ast
GIHUFO	**G**host **I**n **HU**man **FO**rm
GILIG	**G**ruesome **I**nvincible **LI**ghtning **G**host
HIGA	**HI**storical **G**hostly **A**pparition
IRG	**I**ncredibly **R**evolting **G**host
MUWAG	**MU**ddy **WA**ters **G**host
NEPGA	**NE**gative **P**rojection of a **G**hostly **A**pparition
PAWOG	**PA**le **WO**bbly **G**host

STKNOG	**ST**inking **KNO**cking **G**host
TIBIG	**TI**ny **BI**ting **G**host
TOHAG	**TO**tally **HA**rmless **G**host
WHIWHI	**WHI**rlwind **WHI**rler

Miscellaneous Listing of
NECESSITOUS EQUIPMENT AND
NOTEWORTHY ORGANIZATIONS

CDEGH — Clinic for the DE-spookification of GhostHunters

CECOCOG — CEntral COmmission for COmbating Ghosts

COCOT — COntact-COmpression Trap

GES — Ghostly Energy Sensor

GHOSID — GHOst-SImulation Disguise

LOAG — List Of All Known Ghosts

NENEB — NEgative-NEutralizer Belt

OFFCOCAG — OFFice for COmbating CAstle Ghosts

RCFCAG — Retention Centre For Criminally Aggressive Ghosts

RICOG — Research Institute for COmbating Ghosts

ROGA — Register Office for Ghostly Apparitions

COMING SOON!

*Turn the page for a goose-bump-producing,
shiver-inducing sneak peek . . .*

A Ghostly Warning

'Who's there?' whispered a scared voice behind the big door.

'It's Hyssop and Company,' answered Hetty Hyssop. 'The ghosthunters.'

'Oh!' The door opened a crack, and a man and a woman peeped out anxiously.

'Mr and Mrs Worm?' asked Tom. 'Hello, may we come in?'

'Hellooooooooo!' breathed Hugo, giving them a friendly wave with his white fingers.

Bang! The door was shut again.

Hetty Hyssop sighed – and pulled the chain once more.

'That's just my assistant, Hugo the ASG!' cried Mrs Hyssop. 'There's no need to worry; just open the door again.'

Animated whispering started up behind the door. Then it opened again.

'Come in,' whispered a small, fat woman. A red ribbon nestled in her grey hair.

'Yes, come in,' whispered the man. 'You must excuse us, but your assistant – um – yes, well, he looks a bit strange.'

'He's a ghost,' said Tom. 'But a perfectly harmless one.'

'Hey, oi am *not* perfectly harmless,' breathed Hugo. 'In fact oi'd say oi . . .'

But he piped down when he saw Hetty Hyssop's stern look.

It wasn't much warmer inside the castle than outside. The high, gloomy entrance hall was lit only by a couple of candles that hung in iron holders attached to the soot-blackened walls.

'Oh, we are so glad you've come,' whispered Mrs Worm, her voice trembling. 'My saucepans all went flying through the air again today. Flying through the air, I tell you!' She gave a small sob and straightened her ribbon.

'Aha!' Hetty Hyssop nodded and looked around. 'Well, the best thing would be for us to move as quickly as possible into a well-heated room – because very few ghosts like warmth – and there you can tell us exactly what's been going on.'

'Oh, then we're probably best off in the old armoury. My husband has set up a little workshop there,' whispered Mrs Worm. 'Come on.'

With short, rapid steps she hurried towards a huge stone staircase. Two suits of armour standing at the foot of it had no arms, and one was missing a leg.

'As you can see, everything's in a dreadful state,' said Mr Worm. 'Since we've been here, I've been busy with restoration. But I've barely finished something when *whoosh!* – it flies through the air. Or spots of mud appear on it all of a sudden. It's terrible.'

'Mud?' Tom cast a glance at the shimmering trail Hugo left on the stony floor. 'You're sure it's not slime?'

'Slime?' Mrs Worm shook her head. 'Ooooh, no. It is mud. But as I said, quite disgusting as well.'

Tom exchanged an enquiring look with Hetty.

'This way, please!' Mrs Worm led them from the staircase into a corridor. Between the narrow windows, vast numbers of lances, spiked maces, swords and other murderous tools hung from the walls.

'That's the Baron's famous weapon collection,'

whispered Mrs Worm. 'Those lances have already flown past our ears several times. One even followed me into the kitchen! It really is a miracle that we've not been skewered yet.'

'Very interesting,' said Hetty Hyssop. 'Oh, and by the way, you don't need to whisper. Most ghosts can't hear particularly well. They smell their victims, which is a highly reliable method, unfortunately enough.'

'Truuuuuuuuuuuuue.' Hugo turned a bluish colour. 'And oi can smell somethiiiiing now. Somethiiiiing old and spoitefool.'

Disconcerted, he wobbled a couple of metres backwards.

Tom quickly rummaged in his rucksack and pulled out a large spray bottle filled with salt water.

'Quick!' cried Hetty Hyssop. 'Against the wall!'

Mr Worm obeyed, but Mrs Worm stood as if rooted to the spot, staring upwards. High on the wall, a gigantic spear was moving against the iron hoops that held it to the wall. Its wooden handle thrashed to and fro like a wooden snake.

Tom squirted a full load of salt water on to it, and the lance went as limp as a piece of rope, but then two maces freed themselves, flew through the air and bored their way into the floor. Soon sabres, spears and lances were all raining down – and, right in the middle of them, Mrs Worm began to giggle.

It was quite a repellent giggle, hoarse and hollow.

And then Mrs Worm's head started to light up like a pumpkin at Halloween. Her face became blurred, as if it were made of liquid. Her eyebrows thickened, green slime dripped from her hair, and her mouth twisted itself into a revolting smile.

'The Baroness!' cried Mr Worm in horror. 'The Bloody Baroness!'

'A bodynapper!' cried Hetty Hyssop. 'Quick, Tom, bite your tongue! You too, Mr Worm!'

'Thiiiiis iiiiis my castle!' hissed Mrs Worm in the spookiest voice Tom had ever heard. 'Go awaaaaay!'

'The salt water, Tom!' cried Hetty Hyssop. 'Squirt some on her feet!'

Tom held the spray bottle at arm's length and squirted all the remaining salt water on to Mrs Worm's feet.

'Eeeeeeeurgh!' wailed the Bloody Baroness. Mrs Worm hopped up and down like crazy as a greenish-grey muddy puddle grew all around her.

'IIIII'll beeee baaaack!' howled the vile voice. Mrs

Worm's face turned normal again, her head stopped glowing, her hair turned back to grey – and the ghost was gone.

'My darling!' Worried, Mr Worm rushed over to his wife.

'She was – *hic!* – inside – *hic!* – me!' sobbed Mrs Worm. 'Oh, it was so – *hic!* – dreadful, absolutely dreadful.'

Her husband took her in his arms to comfort her.

'And now – *hic!* – I've – *hic!* – got hiccups as well!' cried Mrs Worm in despair.

'Don't worry!' said Hetty Hyssop. 'It will pass after about twenty-four hours. That's a typical consequence of a bodynapper attack.'

'Twenty – *hic!* – four – *hic!* – hours!' cried Mrs Worm, and was overcome by such a violent attack of the hiccups that she couldn't utter another sound.

'Hugo!' cried Tom. 'Hugo, for goodness' sake, where have you got to?'

'Here!' Grinning, Hugo wobbled out of a suit of armour. 'Hey, that was quoite sometheengg, eh? A real ghostly arteest. Impresseeve. Really impresseeve, don't you agreeeeee?'

'Well, I think I can just about resist the attraction!' said Tom. 'Can you still smell something?'

Hugo sniffed and shook his head. 'Gone!' he said disconsolately. 'Moiles away!'

Hetty Hyssop nodded. 'Yes, it's still light, and most ghosts can't manage much haunting when it's light. Let's make the most of it! I hope it's not much further to the armoury.'

Mr Worm shook his head.

'OK, then, let's go.'

The Worms, their legs trembling, led the ghost-hunters farther through the dark castle.

'My dear Tom,' whispered Hetty Hyssop as they followed the couple, 'that's one powerful opponent. Powerful and malicious. I fear we've got an uncomfortable night ahead of us. What do you think?'

Unfortunately, Tom could only agree.

Do you have what it takes to be a
GHOSTHUNTER?

Visit
www.CorneliaFunkeFans.com
to find out!

Click on FUN STUFF & then
GHOSTHUNTERS to:

Have the slime of your life with the
ghastly GHOSTHUNTING GAME

Test your specialist ghoul-edge with the
OFFICIAL GHOSTHUNTERS EXAMINATION

Ghost-write messages to your pals with the
SPOOK-PROOF SECRET MESSAGE DECODER

Read a phantom-astic exclusive
INTERVIEW WITH HETTY HYSSOP

Have a gooey-go at a SPOOK-U-DO,
WORDSEARCH, and more!

Find out about other spectre-tacular books in the
GHOSTHUNTERS series coming out in July 2007

GHOSTHUNTERS and the Incredibly Revolting Ghost!
GHOSTHUNTERS and the Bloodthirsty Baroness!
GHOSTHUNTERS and the Mud-Dripping Monster!